The Story of
ESTHER
A PURIM TALE

Retold by Eric A. Kimmel

Illustrated by Jill Weber

Holiday House / New York

For Gabi and Maytal—E. A. K.

For Rainer, a powerful woman to be—J. W.

Text copyright © 2011 by Eric A. Kimmel

Illustrations copyright © 2011 by Jill Weber

All Rights Reserved

HOLIDAY HOUSE is registered in the U.S. Patent and Trademark Office.

Printed and bound in September 2010 at Kwong Fat Offset Co., Ltd., Dongguan City,

Quang Dong Province, China.

The text typeface is Weiss Medium.

The artwork was created with a combination of acrylic, gouache, tempera,

and brilliant watercolor inks with a little bit of pencil.

www.holidayhouse.com

First Edition

1 3 5 7 9 10 8 6 4 2

Library of Congress Cataloging-in-Publication Data

Kimmel, Eric A.

The story of Esther / retold by Eric A. Kimmel ; illustrated by Jill Weber. — 1st ed.

p. cm.

ISBN 978-0-8234-2223-4 (hardcover)

1. Esther, Queen of Persia—Juvenile literature.

2. Bible stories, English—O.T. Esther. I. Title.

BS580.E8K56 2010

222'.909505—dc22

2008048490

It happened in the days of Ahasuerus, king of Persia, who ruled from India to the Ethiopian highlands.

One night the king held a banquet in his palace in the capital city of Shushan. The noble lords and ladies of Persia all attended. Except one.

"Where is Vashti?" Ahasuerus asked. He sent a messenger with an order for the queen to come to the banquet at once. The messenger returned without her, saying, "The queen is ill. She refuses to come."

"How dare she refuse the king's command!" Ahasuerus shouted. "Vashti is unworthy to be queen. She will be queen no more." The king sent Vashti away in disgrace.

Months passed. King Ahasuerus decided to marry again. He summoned all the maidens in the land of Persia to the city of Shushan. One would be chosen to become his queen.

Now at this time there was a man named Mordecai living in the city of Shushan. He was a Hebrew, descended from those carried off as captives years ago, when the Babylonian king Nebuchadnezzar burned the city of Jerusalem and destroyed the Holy Temple. Mordecai had a niece, Hadassah. The Persians called her Esther, the Morning Star, for in their eyes she was as beautiful as the Queen of Heaven.

Mordecai brought Esther to the king's palace. She did not want to go. "What if the king commands me to do something against my religion?" she asked her uncle.

"If that happens, you must refuse," Mordecai said. "However, it may not come to that. The Persians do not pray to idols. King Ahasuerus has always allowed us to worship in our own way. Do your best to serve him. If he asks about your people and your religion, tell the truth. But if he does not ask, there is no need to speak of it. Above all, do not be afraid. Trust God to protect you and to help you to find favor in the king's eyes."

Esther entered the palace. Mordecai waited in the courtyard. He came there every day, asking those who passed through the gates about Esther and how she fared.

One day while sitting by the gate, he overheard two royal guards talking. They spoke openly, thinking that Mordecai, a Hebrew, would not know what they were saying. However, Mordecai understood Persian. He listened as the guards plotted to murder the king.

Mordecai revealed the plot to the king's officers. The treacherous guards were arrested. The officers thanked Mordecai for saving the king's life.

Meanwhile, inside the palace, the maidens prepared themselves to meet the king. Each strove to become the most beautiful. They bathed in milk and perfumed themselves with costly scents. They dressed in exquisite gowns and put on priceless jewelry. They darkened their eyelids with kohl and reddened their lips with cinnabar.

Esther added but a touch of color
to her face. Her only jewelry was a pair of
gold earrings. She dressed in a simple gown
of Egyptian linen. While the other maidens
piled their hair into towering structures of
netting and wires, Esther combed her hair
and tied it with a cord of white wool.

The other maidens laughed to see
her dressed so simply. But King Ahasuerus
did not laugh when Esther came before him.
Esther's natural beauty outshone the others as the
full moon outshines the stars and the planets. When
the king spoke to her, she answered with such wit that
he thought, "She is one in ten thousand. I am a fool if I do
not make this girl my queen."

King Ahasuerus announced his choice. Esther became his bride and took Vashti's place as queen of all Persia.

Soon after these events, the king's chief minister, Haman, the son of Hammedatha, came riding toward the palace gate. His servants cried, "Bow down to Haman! Bow to the living god!"

The people in the street rushed to throw themselves on the ground. Only one remained standing: Mordecai, Esther's uncle. Haman's guards tried to force him to his knees. Mordecai was stronger than they were. He threw them aside as if they were toys.

"Why won't you bow to me, the king's minister?" Haman asked.

"I will gladly bow to you as the king's minister," Mordecai said. "But I will never bow to you as god. There is only one God, who made heaven and earth. That God alone do I worship."

Haman's anger flared. He vowed to take revenge on Mordecai, his family, and his entire people.

That evening Haman whispered to King Ahasuerus,
"Are you aware that there are a people living in your land who
ignore your laws and insult your officials? They call themselves Hebrews,
for it is said their ancestors came from the other side of the Great River.
They cannot be trusted. It is best to get rid of them now, every one, lest
they rise up in time of war and join your enemies."

"Do as you think best," King Ahasuerus said, handing Haman his
signet ring engraved with the royal seal.

Haman wrote out a proclamation and stamped it with the king's
own seal. He sent copies to all the governors and officials in every
corner of the land, telling them that on the thirteenth day of the
twelfth month, which is called Adar, every Hebrew within their
walls, gates, and borders was to be killed. Neither the old nor the
young was to be spared.

The proclamation puzzled the people of Shushan. "Why does the king hate the Hebrews?" they wondered. "They have lived among us for years. They have harmed no one. They are our friends and neighbors." But a proclamation stamped with the king's seal was law. No one could question it.

Mordecai tore his clothes. He poured ashes on his head. Dressed in rags, he went to sit by the palace gate.

Esther's servants noticed him there and informed the queen. She came out to speak with her uncle. Mordecai read Haman's proclamation to her. "You must go to the king. Beg him to spare the lives of our people."

"I cannot," Esther said. "No one—not even the queen—may approach the king without permission. I cannot go unless he summons me. It is death to do so."

Mordecai answered. "Do you think you will be safe in your palace while your people perish? I believe that God will save us. If not through you then surely through someone else."

"I will do what you ask," said Esther. "Have our people pray for me. I will go to the king, even if it means my death."

Esther dressed in her finest robes. With the royal crown on her head, she went to stand silently at the entrance to the king's throne room. The king noticed Esther standing in the doorway. He smiled and pointed his scepter toward her, inviting her to enter. Esther bowed, then touched the scepter with her fingertip.

"What may I do for my queen?"
King Ahasuerus said. "Ask, and
you will receive, even if it were
half my realm."

"I desire only your happiness,"
Esther replied. "I know the cares of
ruling are heavy. I have arranged a feast
to gladden your heart. Please come to
my chamber tomorrow night. Bring
your minister, Haman, with you."

Haman's pride swelled like never before. He boasted to his wife, "The queen has invited me to a private feast with the king. Next to King Ahasuerus, I am the greatest in the land. Yet my joy turns bitter when I see that rascal Mordecai sitting by the palace gate."

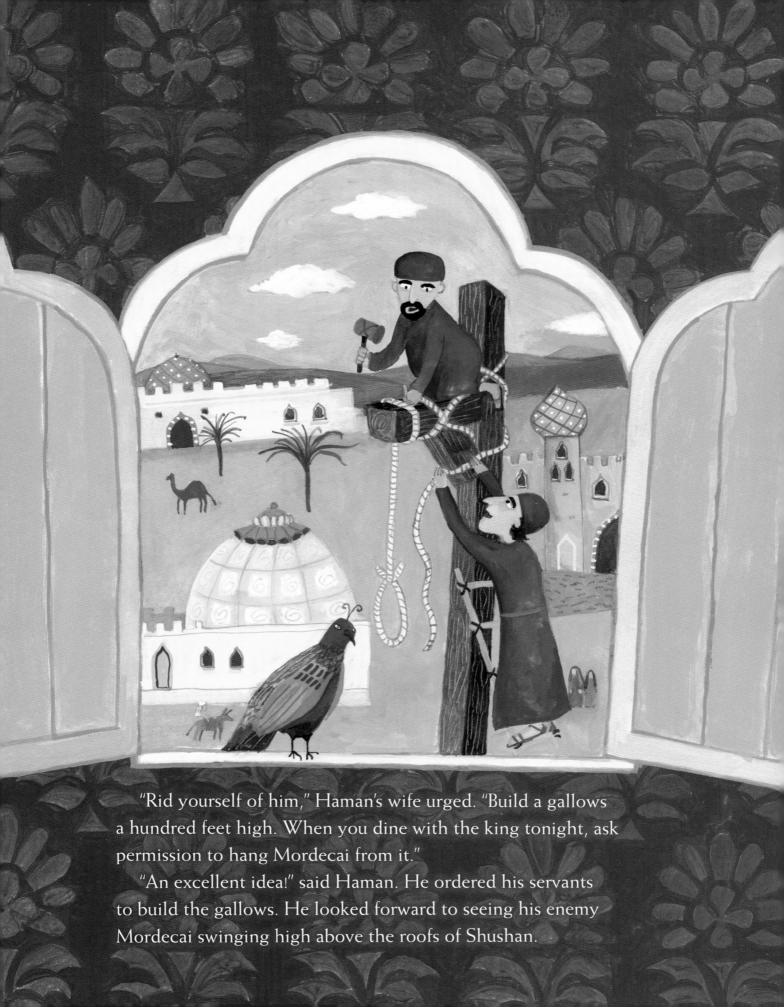

"Rid yourself of him," Haman's wife urged. "Build a gallows a hundred feet high. When you dine with the king tonight, ask permission to hang Mordecai from it."

"An excellent idea!" said Haman. He ordered his servants to build the gallows. He looked forward to seeing his enemy Mordecai swinging high above the roofs of Shushan.

That night King Ahasuerus could not sleep. He summoned his scribes to read to him from the royal chronicles. The scribes read how Mordecai the Hebrew warned the king of the guards' treachery.

"This man saved my life," said King Ahasuerus. "How was he rewarded?"

"No reward was ever given," the scribes answered.

"This cannot be," said the king. "A man who saves the king's life must be rewarded. Send for my minister, Haman."

When Haman arrived, King Ahasuerus asked him, "What should be done for the man whom the king wishes to honor?"

Haman flushed with pride. He thought the king wanted to honor him. "Your Majesty," he began, "this man must be dressed in a royal robe with a royal crown on his head. He must be mounted on the finest horse in your stables. Your most important minister should lead him through the city, crying out so all may hear, 'Behold the man whom the king wishes to honor!'"

"Excellent!" King Ahasuerus exclaimed. "Do this for Mordecai, the man who sits at the palace gates. You yourself shall lead him."

So Mordecai was dressed in a royal robe. A golden crown was placed upon his head. He was mounted on a white horse from the royal stables. Haman, the king's minister, led him through the streets of Shushan, crying out, "Behold the man whom the king wishes to honor!"

Haman's hatred for Mordecai and his people knew no bounds. At the same time, when the people of Shushan saw Mordecai raised up and Haman brought low, they began to wonder if Haman might be less powerful than he claimed.

Haman and King Ahasuerus attended Esther's banquet the following night. Haman practiced the words he meant to say. When the king was merriest, he intended to ask permission to hang Mordecai. But as he started to speak, King Ahasuerus turned to Esther. "My beloved queen," he began, "thank you for this fine feast. I have never enjoyed myself as I have tonight. Let me grant you a gift. Ask for whatever you desire."

Esther threw herself at the king's feet. Trembling, she grasped his hand and begged, "My lord and husband, spare my life. Spare the lives of my uncle Mordecai and my people. Do not allow our enemies to destroy us."

"Who threatens my beloved queen? Who would kill my loyal friend Mordecai?" King Ahasuerus shouted.

Esther pointed to Haman. "That man!
Haman, your minister!"

She thrust a copy of Haman's
proclamation into his hands.

King Ahasuerus read it with growing rage.

"How dare you!" he shrieked at Haman.

"This proclamation is a forgery! You misused
the power I gave you!"

In terror, Haman clasped Esther's feet. "O Queen! Have mercy!
Spare my life!"

King Ahasuerus kicked him away. "How dare you touch the queen!
Away with this wretch! Hang him from that gallows out there! Hang
his whole family with him!"

And so the end that Haman prepared for Mordecai became his own. King Ahasuerus canceled Haman's proclamation, decreeing instead that Mordecai and his people should be honored and protected. Furthermore, from that time forth, the thirteenth day of Adar would be a celebration for the Hebrews and their neighbors as well.

So it is to this day. The thirteenth day of Adar is a time of joy and merriment. And because Haman threw dice to choose the day of destruction, the holiday is named after the Persian word for dice: *pur*.

That is why we call it Purim.